The House on the Edge of Homerville

Walter Foster

Published by Walter Foster, 2023.

THE HOUSE ON THE EDGE OF HOMERVILLE

First edition. January 31, 2023.

Copyright © 2023 Walter Foster.

ISBN: 979-8215406793

Written by Walter Foster.

Also by Walter Foster

Blackula the Vampire!
Tour of Atlantis
The House on the Edge of Homerville
Blackenstein
FRAGMENTS: abort Martian landing!

to jeremy

The HOUSE
on the Edge
of Homerville
by
Walt Foster

The House

O*n the EDGE*
of
Homerville
Chapter
One

Baltimore, Md.
September, 2016

He had murdered his wife.

He didn't mean to do it. He couldn't control himself. She had come home late. There was an argument. He struck her. *Maliciously! Purposefully!* She fell and hit her head on the table. But he didn't stop there. He strangled her, with his bare hands! He just lost it! It was just one of those things! He accused her of seeing someone else. Before he knew what had happened, he was out of the door.

He regretted it.

. . . They gave him fifty years.

He was already thirty eight. He left the court room, his hands in front of him in shackles. As he left the court room, he had the look of shock on his face. Somehow, he thought they'd go lighter on him. His defense made it plain:

'Temporary insanity! He didn't know what he was doing!' they yelled, to anyone who would listen.

But the State would not hear of it. They wanted him prosecuted to the full extent of the law. It had been a high profile case, followed in the national press for months as the trial lingered on.

Outside the court room in the hallways, the verdict in, the news hounds fell over each other trying to get their pictures or his statement. Microphones were in his face. The uniformed police had to hold them off.

The media was resilient.

"Are you going to appeal?" asked one reporter.

"I'm innocent," said the man, showing them his wrist shackles.

"The evidence point otherwise," said another reporter.

"Involuntary manslaughter. We're going to appeal," said his lawyer, holding onto his client.

They were trying to make their way outside.

The press continued to hound them until they were out to the street and to their waiting car. The Baltimore police put him into the back seat of one of their black and white units. One of the officers climbed into the drivers seat and the man was taken away, the bevy of reporters left standing at the curve.

Things had never been easy for thirty eight year old Frank Bonner. People say he was born on the wrong side of the tracks. He never had much, his mother was pregnant with him when she was sixteen. He never knew his father; never had the guidance of a *strong* male figure in his life. He dropped out of school when he was in the nineth grade. He wondered from mediocre job to mediocre job.

Then, he was arrested for shoplifting at a local grocery store. His mother was at his side and supported him during the weekend he served for the act. **Then,** at knife point, he robbed a convenience store.

He served six months.

Then, he stole a car right off the dealers lot; hot wired it and drove away. He was captured in less than an hour. He did another four months in jail.

The outside world didn't greet him with 'open arms' in any event after he had paid his debt to society. He had a rap sheet a mile long. He promised his mother he would do better. Nothing she did seemed to work.

Then, he found a job working in an auto shop as a mechanic. He'd always loved cars; loved being around them; loved tinkering with them. Though he had only a nineth grade education he was good at fixing and repairing them. He figured, 'everybody has *some* talent!;

maybe this was HIS!' He just picked it up!; from his neighbors and his neighbors friends while in his teens and early twenties.

The job paid well; two dollars per hour, eight hours per day plus benefits. For the first time Bonner seemed settled.

Then he met a girl, a night club singer, fell in love and married her inside of two months. It was a whirlwind romance and indeed all seemed to be going well for him.

One night, however, she came in late. She had been delayed. She had no explanation. They got into an argument. He thought she should have been home earlier. She brandished a knife on him. He took it from her and brandished it at her, but he did more; he threw the knife away, beat her and strangled her with his bare hands.

He had been drinking and was caught up in the moment.

He ran from the scene.

It was easy for the law. He was picked up a short time later having a casual drink at a local bar as if nothing had happened.

He didn't realize the seriousness of it all. He went quietly with the authorities, without further incident.

The case was open and shut.

Frank Bonner was slated to spend the rest of his life in prison. He spent ten hours per day in an eight by ten cell and fourteen hours per day working in the prison library, with one day out for recreation into the prison yard, Saturday, all under heavy guard. He thought: it was 'hardly' an ideal existance.

Chapter

Two

...Until he escaped!!!

A*fter eight* months, Frank grew weary of the prison walls and devised a plan!

Frank Bonner was not a large man. He only stood about five feet seven in his shoes and weighed one hundred and sixty pounds. Most of the prisoners were much larger; much bulkier.

On one of his Saturday outings he noticed the building was made of concrete 'blocks' and they coincided next to the giant coolers and heaters that cooled off or heated the facility. The coolers were right next to his cell which *hid* it somewhat from the tower. While the guards looked away he briefly ducked behind one of the large coolers. He realized that the blocks were 'staggered' and gave way to tiny vents that opened to each cell. He realized again that

there was a vent in his own cell as well. Therefore, he thought, there

were 'two' vents: one on the inside of the cell, and one on the

'outside'. He needed only to find some way to get through *both* vents

to be on the outside.

Bonner's mind began to work.

AND HE ASKED HIMSELF: "How would it work?'

At night, the prison guard tower had a search light that passed over the outside area about once every five minutes and lit up the area for many yards like day. It's beacon could see in all directions for half a mile and the tower was always manned, even in the daytime. Dogs roamed the area that separated the prison itself from a ten foot high wired fence, from about ten p.m. until dawn. Two feet high barbed wire coiling was at the top of all fences.

The prison was a fortress, and Bonner knew it.

But Bonner wasn't discouraged, nor was he intimidated.

Then, as he took dinner one evening the answer came

to him! He stared at his *fork* and *knife*. The nuts on the vent had a

'certain' kind of *top,* one he thought he could devise with the knife and fork he had in his hand. As the two hundred or so prisoners had

their dinner, no one paid much attention to him as he slipped both

utensils into his pocket. The guard nearest him was looking the other

way. He put two slabs of meat into his pocket also; those were for

the dogs outside.

When dinner was over, he lined up in single file behind the others and was led to his cell, his utensils firmly hidden away.

It would take *weeks* but he carved the knife point into the design of the top of the screws. He used the 'back end' of the fork as a chisel to make his design on the *front* end of the knife. The front of the knife soon matched *perfectly* with the top of the screws! He would use the sharp end of the fork to fit over the top end of the knife like a 'ratchet', a system he once used for cars, to 'pivot' the knife on the screw.

On the same night after the guard had made his patrol past his cell, Bonner began to turn the screws to test his device. It wasn't easy. It was usually quiet and the twisting of the screws made more noise than he had wanted it to. The sweat was popping off his face as he worked. As he turned, the knife continued to slip the bolt.

He kept trying.

He could hear the slow 'tap-tap-tap' of the prison guard returning outside his cell in the hallway. He ran back to his bunk, stuffed the utensils under his mattress and climbed in. He picked up a magazine and pretended to read. The guard peeped in briefly, but turned away and kept walking.

Bonner climbed from his bed and took the makeshift ratchet set from under the mattress. He continued to work, digging in deeper and deeper into the stubborn screw.

Finally, after much effort the screw turned! It was unbelievable! He seemed relieved but immediately went after the second of four screws, using the fork at the top of the knife for leverage.

He turned the screw. *It loosened!*

He went after the third screw. And after some effort, it to, loosened. He didn't bother to open the fourth screw. He simply bent the vent 'downwards.'

He had one more hurdle. There was a *second* outside vent similiar to the one he had just loosened. The screws were on the outside! Bonner had no recourse.

As the footsteps of the lone guard faded in the distance down the hall he managed to kick in with his feet the outside vent and it gave way!

HE POSITIONED HIMSELF the other way. He was amazed! After living so close to the vent itself he could see to the *outside* so plainly.

He crawled up a few inches and peeped outwards and could see the huge block heaters next to the vent exit. He wasted no time. He had put the meat under his bed onto the floor. He came back to the cell, grabbed it and put it through the hole to the outside. It took some effort and repositioning but soon he was on the outside!; And in the exact spot he had calculated! And he was in the shadow of the coolers, not to be plainly seen! He kept *low* and behind the giant box-like wind blowers and heaters. Dogs were in the area and he didn't want to be seen by the spotlight which roamed up and down the otherwise quiet yard. Any activity at that hour would be pounced on like a wolf on prey, by either the guards or the canines.

That much he knew!

The dogs were congregated and sleeping in an large area on the other side of the basketball court about fifty feet away from where he was.

After a moment or two, the spot light swooped in, in the vacinity of the coolers and again he ducked down low to avoid detection. When the light went by him he stood, reached into to the ground and picked up two slabs of meat. He stood out from the cooler and threw them fifty yards from where he was standing and the dogs pounced on it.

The diversion had been created! The spot light immediately went to where the dogs were, as they were fighting for a slice of the meat.

In the confusion, Bonner made a mad dash for the

ten foot prison fence, climbing atop of it and maneuvering his way

through the coiled barbed wire. He cut himself many times on his

arms and legs, drawing blood, but slowly he began to emerge on the

outside of the wire, the red pricks covering all over his body. He saw

the guards rush out to the dogs to see what the disturbance was as the

light shinned on them.

Bonner had made it through. He climbed down the other side of the fence making an agonizing noise of pain in his desperation. One guard on the ground saw him and began blowing his whistle.

The guard fired a shot into the air.

"Stop you!"

Bonner started to run. Other guards came out of the building. The first guard ran towards the fence and the dogs followed him. There were a total of ten guards on night duty. The same guard fired another shot over Bonner's head as he reached the fence.

He yelled again at him. "I said stop!"

Bonner kept running. The search light was just getting to him. It saw him making his way across tall grass on his way to some nearby woods.

The guard fired again, but not into the air; but by then Bonner was too far away. The two guards in the tower began firing at will, each missing as Bonner weaved back and forth. Momentarily, he had disappeared into the woods.

The guard who had reached the fence first opened the gate with a key, and with a rifle raised he began a hot pursuit of Bonner. The bevy of other armed guards, some with rifles as well, joined in the pursuit. They had dogs. The spotlight continued to shine into the place in the woods Bonner had entered. But Bonner himself was too long gone.

A general alarm with *flashing red lights* twirling,

meaning prison break, was going off all over the place and on top of

the bob-wired fence. The ten or so guards reached the woods; the

woods itself lit up like daylight by the steady beacon from the guard

tower.

Chapter

Three

W_ith their_ rifles butts they beat back brush in order to find him. The blood hounds, however, picked up his trail handily and within a few moments they had an accurate account on where he was headed.

The road!

Bonner kept moving. Desperation was all over his face. He could hear the dogs behind him.

Then, he heard a noise.

It was traffic! Cars! He was near a road! And it wasn't far away!

He could see the headlights. He knew that there was a highway there but he didn't think he was that close! The cars seemed closer than the dogs! He wondered how he would get the dogs to stop. He had no meat.

Within a few moments he had reached the road.

Again, his mind began to devise a clever plan. He would sacrifice himself, lay on the road and _force_ someone to stop. He stretched out in the right lane. Sure enough, a truck came by and the driver slammed on his brakes.

Bonner got up and rushed to the drivers side of the truck. He put his hands into the inside of his shirt and pointed it at the driver, an elderly man.

"Move over! Move over or I'll let you have it!" Bonner yelled at him.

The driver put his hands high and moved over to the other side of the truck. Bonner jumped into the drivers seat and began to drive away screeching his tires as he did.

The guards and dogs reached the road at about the same time and they fired their weapons into the air, more out of frustration, than an attempt to stop them.

The first guard held up his hands.

"Stop! They're gone! We don't want to wake up the whole neighborhood or hurt a civilian!" he said, pushing down the rifle of a guard.

He looked at all the guards. "We'll put out an APB. Did any of you get a good look at that truck?"

The guards all agreed that they did.

The guard looked at the red tail lights still speeding away. "We'll get him; planes; dogs; helicopters; whatever means, we'll get him."

The guards turned and headed back.

Chapter
Four

Bonner drove the truck with one hand. He held the other under his shirt.

He looked over at the obviously frightened man.

"We're about the same size, ain't we?" he asked him.

"Looks like it," the man said, his hands still held up high.

Bonner pulled to the side of the road.

He pointed his finger under his shirt at the man.

"Get out of the truck," he told the man.

The man still had his hands up.

"What?"

"I said, get out of the truck!" Bonner said, his voice sounding more desparate than ever.

"What you gonna do?" the man asked climbing out.

Bonner came around to the front side of ther truck and looked at the man.

"Yeah, you'll do. Get outta them things," he said to the man.

"What? I'll freeze!"

"You'll have these," Bonner said, referring to his clothes.

The man looked him over as if for the first time.

"Wait a minute; that color', that stripe down the side - "

He looked at Bonner. "Them's prison clothes!"

"Well, what do you expect stupid? I'm a prisoner, ain't I? Now get outta them things!" Bonner yelled.

The man began to undress and soon was down to his underwear.

Bonner reached out with his free hand. "Throw 'em to me!"

The man tossed his clothes to Bonner and Bonner tossed his to the man. Bonner hid on the other side of the truck so the man could not see him. He put on the man's clothes. He came around to the front of the truck, put his hands underneath his shirt and stuck it out at the man. "Go ahead! Put 'em on!"

The man was hesitant. But slowly he deemed it necessary to cooperate. He put on the prison clothes.

Bonner looked at himself. "Now I look like anybody else, don't I? Thanks!"

He looked at the man. "Got any money?"

"In the back pocket," the man said.

With his free hand Bonner pulled out the man's wallet. He handily searched it's contents.

He showed it to the man. "I'll say you do. You're loaded. That is to say, I am."

He put the wallet back into his pocket. "Now back away."

The man put up his hands.

Bonner finally pulled out his hand from under his shirt.

It was empty.

He grinned at the man, winked at him and pointed his finger at his head. *"Bang!"*

He turned and made a mad dash for the drivers seat of the truck. He climbed in and drove away, leaving the man stranded, alone on the side of the road.

Chapter

Five

He knew they had seen the truck.

They had almost reached it as he drove away. He knew he had to ditch it; *somewhere;* that somehow by land, sea or air, they'd be looking for it.

Baltimore was a big city, he thought. It was full of people. He thought perhaps he could lose himself there! He kept driving. It seemed every police car he passed was chasing him.

He kept driving.

Soon, a sign said Baltimore City Limits. In his own mind, that would be as good as he could have it. 'Yes,' he thought, 'perhaps he *could* lose himself here.' He was already starting to see lots and lots of people!

Though he was from the city itself, he couldn't exactly recall where the bus station was. He saw a man walking down the street. He pulled to the side and flagged him. "Hey! How far is bus station?"

"Two blocks down, make a right on the Juniper Street, then left on Eighth. It's on Eighth street," the man said.

"Thanks," Bonner said.

He turned back onto the street and drove away.

He drove away from the bus station, however: far away. He estimated he was at least a mile from the bus station when he parked. He was from Baltimore but had forgotten how big it really was.

He abandoned the truck. He didn't want the authorities to assume he had taken a bus. So he walked, losing himself in the shoulder to shoulder of the downtown crowd as he hurried towards the bus station. He simply wanted to get out of town, and fast! It didn't seem to matter where he was going!

It took him about an hour to walk through the crowded streets to the bus terminal.

Finally, there it was, the bus terminal, as crowded as the streets. There was a man sitting in a chair behind the glass window.

Watching his every step, Bonner approached the window. "When is your next bus leaving?"

"Where do you want to go, Sir?" the man asked.

"It doesn't matter! I mean - "

He looked up at the board behind the man. He chose the very first departure on the list. "New Orleans! That's it! New Orleans!"

He continued to look over his shoulder. "I've always wanted to go there!"

"Is that where you want to go now?" the man asked.

"Yes, give me a ticket! And hurry!" Bonner cried.

The man began to look at his records.

"Round trip or one way?"

"One way."

A police car passed by slowly on the street outside and Bonner ducked down low. When the car had completely gone by he stood up straight again. "Could you step on it buddy?"

"Relax, pal," the man said. "The bus doesn't leave for thirty minutes."

The man stamped the ticket. "Twenty dollars."

Bonner reached into his pocket and took from it twenty of the dollars he had taken from the man in the truck. He noticed he had only thirty dollars left; not much, he thought, to have in a big city like New Orleans.

He gave the man the ticket fare. The man handed him the ticket. "Have a nice trip!"

"Thanks," Bonner said.

The bus station was comprised of four floors.

LEVEL ONE WAS INBOUND buses coming in from all points north and west.

Level two was inbound buses coming in from all points south and east.

Level three was outbound buses going all points north and east.

And level four was outbound buses going to all points south and west.

He was headed for New Orleans; level four.

He went to the stairs to climb the four levels to his departure. He felt a sense of elation. He had fooled the authorities. He was almost out of town!

On his way up the stairs he passed a security guard. Bonner turned away and hid his face. He kept walking. He kept moving up to level four.

Level four was very crowded. There were people

sitting, at the snack bar or talking on the public phones. He took

a seat. He had no luggage and attempted to have a low profile. No

one payed much attention to him. The minutes to boarding passed

by slowly.

A uniformed man soon came to the front of the bus.
He began yelling:
"Boarding! Charlotte; Columbia; Atlanta; Birmingham; Jackson; Lake Charles; New Orleans; ALL ABOARD!"

Bonner quickly got up and got in line. He was among the first to line up. Before too long he had claimed his seat, near the rear. Within a short time the driver climbed on and the bus began to back out of it's stall. He honked his horn as he left and the bus began to roll forward.

A sigh of relief came over his face. He had made it. He had made it out of Baltimore! He leaned back into his seat and wiped the sweat from his face. He even took a nap. He had been running all day. It was the first peaceful moment he had had in many hours.

When he awakened he noticed a man a few seats ahead of him reading the headlines.

'MAN ESCAPES FROM PRISON'

The headlines read.

There was even a picture of him, right on the front page.

Bonner slipped down a little more into his seat. He pulled up his shirt on the passenger side of him to further disquise his face. He dared not make eye contact with anyone. He just wanted to get out of town; to put distance between himself and his ordeal! In his mind, he had done just that.

'Good,' he thought. 'Good.'

He took another nap.

Chapter
Six

He *was* awakened by the hawking of the driver yelling:

"Homerville!"

Bonner stretched and wiped his eyes. By this time it was the next night.

He looked out at the terrian.

'Homerville?' he thought.

He shook the grogginess out of his head and looked outside again. The town was obviously small. He thought that there were many small towns in America along the route he was headed, many of which he knew outside Baltimore. But he had never heard of Homerville before and there was no mention of it before he boarded.

The driver hawked again: *"Homerville. Thirty minute rest stop. Thirty minutes," he said.*

Bonner was confused.

The driver stepped to the bottom of the steps and started helping passengers off.

Bonner looked around at the other passengers as they left. They were filing off as if they knew where they were. After the thirty or so passengers had disembarked the bus the driver climbed back on and began doing to what appeared some paperwork.

From the back of the bus Bonner looked at him.

"Excuse me, Sir?" Bonner asked.

The driver looked to the back at him.

"Yes, Sir," he asked.

"What did you say the name of this town was?"

"Homerville, Son. Thirty minute rest stop. Better hurry," he driver said.

The driver turned and stepped off the bus. He disappeared into the small bus terminal.

Bonner was left alone, more confused than ever.

'Homerville?' he thought.

Where was it? What state? What county? He looked outside again and saw people going about their way as if they knew where they were.

He shrugged his shoulders. It was a small town he thought, one light, a few buildings that were lit at that evening hour. But all in all, he thought, it was *somewhere.* After all, he thought, 'who would catch him here?'

He decided to get off the bus. He had thirty minutes to see the sights, few as they were.

He climbed from the bus and thought he would get himself something to drink. But a little diner caught his attention out of the corner of his eye about a block from the terminal.

The diner was small and quaint looking. He knew it was open by it's flashing neon sign outside. He could see people inside from the distance. He decided to go there to refresh himself; perhaps some coffee.

He walked to the counter and sat.

A waitress greeted him friendlily.

"Hi. Welcome to The Diner. What will you have?" she asked, with her pad and pen in her hands.

"Just coffee," Bonner said.

She walked away and poured him a cup and sat it in front of him.

"I just made it. I think you'll like it."

There were four of five other patrons seated at their tables, scattered about here and there. No one paid much attention to him; except the waitress, who stared at him. "Will that be all?"

"Yes," he said, not looking at her.

She gave him a curious look.

"What about a shave?"

". . . What?"

"A shave? You look like you could use one," she said, leaning on the counter.

Bonner touched his chin.

"Yeah. I guess so. But I don't have time. I'm waiting for the bus. I've been riding for almost two days," he said.

"Lots of people come through here with that same problem," she said.

She stood up straight. "We have an agreement with the station. There is some blades in the bathroom, just to the left. I know one of the men that works here; keeps them in a little cabinet above the sink. I don't think he'd mind."

"I guess I forgot mine," he said.

"Don't matter. Go ahead," she said.

"What's your name?"

"It's Sally."

"Thanks, Sally."

Bonner stood up and used her instructions to find the bathroom. He returned, clean and shaven. He sat at the counter again.

He looked at his waitress. "More coffee."

She came over for a closer look at him.

"Now that's more like it; just wanted to see how you looked without all that stubble," she said.

"Do you approve?"

She gave the thumbs up and poured him more coffee.

"I approve. Better hurry or you'll miss your bus," she said.

"Yeah. By the way, you're very nice," he said.

"Thanks," she said.

She walked away to see other customers. He sipped his coffee and prepared to return to the bus.

After about five minutes he decided it was time to go. He turned the final few drops of coffee to his head, reached into his pocket and layed twenty cents on the counter.

And a dime tip for the kind waitress.

As he turned from the counter he noticed a little man sitting at the counter two seats over from him. Bonner seemed to notice him for the first time.

Bonner nodded his head politely at the man and started out.

The little man pointed at him.

"Mind if I sat down young fellow?" the man asked.

He was an older man; much older than Bonner and he was obviously of much shorter stature. His head was completely white; greying all over and he was neatly dressed in a suit.

"No, help yourself," Bonner said, swiveling out his stool from the counter. "I was just leaving."

He took a step towards the door.

The little man stopped him.

"Don't go just yet. Please," the man said, staring at him.

"I'm sorry. What?" Bonner asked the man.

The man sat in the counter stool next to Bonner.

"Please. It could be well worth your while, what I have to say," the man pleaded.

Bonner sat down next to the man.

"As long as you say it real fast! I have a bus to catch!" Bonner said.

"You're not getting on that bus - "

"What?"

". . . Not if you're smart."

The little man turned his chair towards the counter. "I couldn't help hearing your conversation with that waitress."

He turned his chair towards Bonner. "How would you like to make five hundred dollars?"

Bonner hesitated for a moment. His eyes became wider.

". . . Five hundred dollars?" he asked, a bit surprised at the suggestion.

"Yes. You look like you could use it. You had to use that lady to get shaven; you're only drinking coffee. But you look strong and robust. It might take that to do what I want you to do," the man said.

Bonner placed his elbows on top of the counter and put his fingers together.

He looked at the little man.

"What do you want me to do?" he asked him.

"I'm sorry, I didn't introduce myself. My name is Cornelious Williams. I am well known is these parts. I am owner of a house about twenty miles from here called *Williams House*. Oh, it's a grand, quaint place; lots of rooms; a back porch; two floors; balconies for each room. However, it is quite old; a bit *dated*," the man said.

"Congratulations. Why are you telling me?"

"I want you to stay there: overnight."

Bonner sat up straight in his seat.

"Let me get this straight: you want me to stay overnight in some castle you have and when I come out you will hand me five hundred dollars?" he asked.

"We will sign the contracts before you go in," the little man said.

"Why? What's it to you? What's in it for you?" Bonner asked.

"Folks say the place is haunted; ghosts; goblins; the works. I warn you, It's isolated. And I'll admit no one has stayed overnight there and survived it since my great grand father way back at the turn of the nineteenth century. They run out or give up. Folks say he doesn't want anybody else to stay there, the place is *his*," he said.

"Why don't you stay there?"

"I have. But people say, you're just his kin and he let you stay there. I want to prove them wrong. I want to prove that there is nothing wrong with *Williams House*. I want an outsider, someone like yourself, to stay there: overnight, to prove to these nonbelievers that there is nothing wrong with *Williams House* and put this silly legend to rest for good! What do you say?" the man asked.

Bonner paused for a moment. He looked in the direction of the bus terminal. He knew he had no more than five minutes before his bus would leave, and only thirty dollars to his name.

Then he thought, he could catch the next bus the next day. So what, he thought, if he missed it, his ticket would still be good.

He had had more complex ways to make a dollar.

"How long do I have to stay you say?" he asked.

"Just overnight. It'll make a statement to me and to the others around here," the little man said.

Bonner looked away then back to the old man.

"How long is overnight?" he asked.

"Eight o'clock at night till eight o'clock the next morning. Twelve hours. And if you come out okay, I'll give you five hundred dollars in cash," the little man said.

Bonner paused some more. It was a small town. He began to wander how many police were there anyway? One? Two?

'It was a slim chance he'd be caught,' he thought.

He began to think: 'It might just be worth the risk.'

He looked back at the man.

"I'll do it, old timer. And you're going to have that money first thing, right?" Bonner asked.

"In cash, at eight o'clock in the morning when you walk out of William House," the man said.

They shook hands under the counter on the deal.

Bonner looked at him.

"One more thing, old timer; how do you know that after you leave I won't spend the night outside? How do you know I won't spend the night in the woods?"

The little man smiled at him.

"You won't. You're not that type."

Bonner looked at the bus back out of the terminal.

He smiled back at the man.

"What next?"

"You come with me. My truck is just outside. I'll take you to my house. I'll give you overnight provisions; blankets, sandwiches, flashlight, all the things you will need until tomorrow morning," the man said.

"Great. By the way, my name is Bonner. That name doesn't mean anything to you, does it?" Bonner asked.

"Why should it?"

"Just thought I'd ask."

The little man stood up. He gestured his hand toward the exit of the diner.

"Shall we, Mr. Bonner?"

Bonner stood up.

"I'm way ahead of you, Mr. Williams," he said.

Bonner had never been one to turn down an honest dollar, or a dishonest one. Besides being brought up on a homicide charge, he had been involved in assault, robbery and car jacking. He thought staying overnight in some old dump was far better than what he had gotten used to.

The men made their way to Mr. Williams' truck. Within moments they were on the way to his house.

Chapter Seven

L*ATER; SEVEN O'CLOCK*
Bonner was treated to a fried chicken dinner at the man's house. It was as if he was a 'guest' and the little man his host.

"How is dinner?" Mr. Williams asked.

"Fine, just fine," Bonner answered.

The man was standing at the kitchen table. Bonner didn't look at him. He continued to eat. He had not expected such a great meal so inexpensively and so soon; twelve hours earlier, he had been running through the woods.

Bonner finally looked at him. "And this is a fine, fine place you live in, Sir."

"Yes," the little man said. He began to wonder around, looking about the place. "I made some wise investments. It has afforded me this house, land and I was able to buy back the house my great, great grandfather once owned."

"The one I'm going to."

"Yes."

He looked at Bonner. "Aren't you interested in what those investments were, Sonny?"

Bonner took a couple of bites on his chicken.

"Well, as long as you pay, Mister, whoever you are, I don't care what business you're in."

He looked at the man still standing. "Now hear this: I want my money promptly at eight o'clock when I walk out of there. You got me?!"

The man went into the living room and picked up a piece of paper.

"This is the contract: the binding form between you and I. When you walk out of that house, promptly at eight o'clock in the morning, the money will be awarded to you - no questions asked," the man said.

"Let me see that."

Bonner took the paper from him and read it. "Seems binding enough. Give me the pen."

The man handed the pen to Bonner. He signed it and handed the pen and contract back to the little man.

"Excellent. Please follow me, Mr. Bonner."

Bonner wiped his mouth with his sleeve and followed the man into the living room.

The man opened a brown bag. "These are items I told you that you will need. Everything is there; food, drink; blankets; everything."

"I see. You've thought of everything, Sir."

"I want to make sure you are comfortable during your overnight stay!"

"Thank you."

"Now if you are ready, I think we should get started. It is after seven thirty and it is about a half an hour drive to Williams House," the man said.

Bonner picked up the brown bag with it's materials. He gestured friendlily to the door.

"After you," he said to the little man.

The little man led the way to the outside and to the truck. He climbed into the drivers side and Bonner, with his bag, into the passenger seat.

During the thirty minute drive Bonner noticed many average looking farm houses along the way. But as they continued to drive he noticed that the farms began to thin out and become fewer and fewer, until the point that they were nonexistant! Indeed, Bonner noticed, the house they were headed, as the man said, was isolated!

Finally, they reached a two story house with a brick bottom and a wooden upstairs. It was very run down as bushes and brush surrounded it and some time stuck out of it's windows.

The little man pulled to a stop and turned off the engine.

He looked at Bonner.

"Welcome to Williams House," he said.

Bonner looked at the house much closer. Then he looked at the man with queer eyes.

"No wonder no one has lived in it for so long. I'm beginning to wonder if five hundred dollars is enough?! But the contract has been signed, and there is nothing more to do about it," Bonner said, continuing to size the place up.

Mr. Williams climbed out of the truck. With his bag, Bonner climbed out of the other side.

Bonner went up for a closer look.

He looked at Mr. Williams in back of him. "And you own this place?"

"Yes."

"Why?"

"I told you it was purchased by me, because my ancestor once lived here."

Bonner walked as little closer to the house.

"Well, I guess that's good a reason as any," he said, looking back at the man.

Mr. Williams came up to him.

"Well, what do you think?"

"The second floor looked as if it is about to cave in into the first floor! The porch is rotten and many planks are missing! The fence is rusty, sagging in many areas and needs mending badly," Bonner said.

He turned to the man. "Nevermind me, will this place last the night?"

"It will. And either way, it's your home for the next twelve hours, Mr. Bonner."

The man turned and headed for the truck. He climbed in and looked at Bonner. "Just remember our agreement, Mr. Bonner. You come out of there a minute earlier than eight o' clock and the deal is off! You'll walk away from here with only a night of free lounging!"

"You call this free? You should be paying me to stay here! Oh, that's right: you are!" Bonner said.

The man started up his engine and turned on his headlights.

"One more thing," the man said.

"And what is that?" Bonner asked.

"Here."

Bonner came back to the truck and the little man handed him something. "It's a watch! I noticed that you wasn't wearing one. Now you can be on time! I want no excuse that you didn't know the exact time. Eight o'clock."

Bonner stuck the watch into his pocket.

"Eight o'clock," he agreed.

"Have a good night, Mr. Bonner," the man said.

"Yeah," Bonner said.

The man backed out of the driveway. Bonner looked at the man's red tail lights as it disappeared into vastness of the isolated area.

He yelled back at the man. "Hah!"

And under his breath he added: "There's a sucker born every minute."

With his bag Bonner turned and walked towards the house.

He first had to get past the broken down, rusted fence.

As he opened it the gate the hinges failed and it collapsed onto the ground.

Bonner looked at it. "Welcome to Williams House."

It was getting darker and later by the minute and he reached into his bag for his flashlight.

He turned it on.

He walked carefully towards the porch. He knew he could encounter anything; snakes; bats; rats.

'It's either you or five hundred dollars,' he said out loud. 'And you know who's going to win that bet. Me.'

He heard a noise. He trained his light in the direction it had come from. In the bush, not more than a few feet away, he saw a rabbit, obviously scared, trying to get away from the scene. That was an encounter he had not expected.

He shoo'd the rabbit away.

The front door was in no better shape than the gate. Time and weather had taken it's toll there to. It was unlocked, off it's hinges and he was able to push it back without much effort. He walked into the house swaying the beacon of his light side to side. Spider webs abounded everywhere.

He saw a long hallway. It was narrow but rooms were on each side. He didn't bother to look into them. At the end of the hallway was an opening; a room, and it was rather large.

As Bonner drew closer he found it had a full sofa, a coffee table and several chairs placed here and there. He noticed the area was dusty and dingy, and spider webs came down from the ceiling just as they had in the hallway.

It was obviously the living room, but to him, it didn't look as if it was a place that offered much comfort.

Upstairs, on the second floor he saw more rooms, one after the other, protected by a safety rail in the hallway. Bonner was not interested in any of it, however. He thought that all he had to do was stay overnight; the contract did not stipulate where. And he wasn't interested in exploring. He thought the dingy first floor was as good as any and decided to stay there and bed down for the night.

He sat his bag on the couch. Dust rose up from it as he dropped it. He reached into his pocket and took out the watch the man had given him. He shinned his beacon on it.

It was nine thirty.

'Another ten and a half hours in this dump,' he said to himself.

He looked around the house again and came to the conclusion that it had not been occupied in years. Decades. He sat the back end of the flashlight on an old coffee table near the couch. The beacon shinned on the ceiling but lit up the whole room. He dusted the dingy couch with his hands and sat there. He felt a little hungry and decided to feast on what the man had prepared.

It had been a long day. He had made it from his cell to freedom. He knew he was a fugitive from justice but he thought that where he was was only temporary. He felt tired. He stretched out on the couch and drempt of the easy five hundred dollars he would collect on his exit from the house.

He fell asleep on that note; a smile on his face. He had come so far, he thought, but he wanted to go further.

Chapter
Eight

He *was* awakened by organ music. He shook his groggy head. He sat up straight on the couch. *'Music?'*

he thought. 'And from what source?'

He wondered, where could it be coming from? There were no neighbors. He hadn't seen a house within five miles of his coming there! He thought he was completely alone!

'How could that be?' he thought.

But the music wasn't coming from any neighbor. He looked upstairs. The music was coming from upstairs! He reached for the flashlight on the table and shinned it on the second floor. The music was definately coming from up there! He broke up a nearby chair to get to one of it's wooden legs.

With the flashlight in his right hand and the wooden leg in the left he made his way upstairs to where the melodious music had come.

Room by room, he listened, opening and closing the door. Then, on a room near the end of the hallway, the music was *louder.* He took the back end of the flashlight as if he was about to use it as a weapon, raised it high and kicked open the door.

THERE, sitting innocently at the organ was a woman.

She was odd looking; long black hair; long black fingernails and

the darkest eyes he had ever seen, even though he was seeing them

from the side. There was a lantern on a nearby dresser and it's lone

flame lit up the entire room.

His first impression was to turn and to go the other way. However, his second impression said to him; it was a woman; a woman! He thought he was supposed to spend the night in the William House: ALONE!

She seemed to not pay attention to him as she continued to hammer out an odd tune, the same tune he had been hearing. He lowered the flashlight he had held up in a 'defensive' position and let her play on.

Finally, she leaned into the organ for the final note, held it and stopped. She didn't look at him. He had a quizzical look on his face.

He took a step in her direction.

"What is this? Who are you?" he could but ask.

"I am Loren," she said.

She finally looked at him.

He seemed even more quizzical. She could talk.

He took another single step towards her. He waved the beacon of the flashlight around the room and then directly at her. As on the first floor, spider webs were everywhere.

He looked at her.

"What are you doing here, out in the middle of nowhere?" he asked her, his words almost stuck in his mouth.

"I am enjoying myself. I love music."

She looked at him a bit closer. "Don't you love music, Frank?"

"Don't call me Frank!" he yelled.

He stopped.

He looked at her closer. "Wait a minute; how did you know my name?"

"I know all about you, Frank. You're nearly six feet tall, you weigh one hundred and sixty pounds and your hometown is Baltimore Maryland."

"How did you know that?"

"I just know," she said.

"No one just knows these things. Mr. Williams told you, didn't he? That land lord. He told you all about me, didn't he?" he asked, anxiously.

"I promise you no one told me anything about you. And what land lord?" she asked.

He took another step into the room.

"What is this, a joke? And I'm the center of it? That's it isn't it? A joke. Well I don't like it! I don't like it at all! I'm not laughing!" he yelled.

He took a small dresser on the side of the room and flung it a couple of paces.

The woman seemed startled.

He looked at her. "That's what I think of about your little joke!"

He shinned the light around the room some more. "Now what? What happens now that I've found you out? And how much are they paying *you*?"

"I don't know what you're talking about, Frank," she said, innocently.

"Stop calling me Frank! I don't know you. And you don't know me!" he yelled.

"Oh, but I *do* know you."

She started playing the same tune on the organ again.

Bonner covered his ears.

"Is that the only tune you know? That's the same song!"

"I haven't put it into words yet. But the words will come. Good writers always write the melody, then the words," she said.

She stood up. Bonner noticed she was an attractive woman, wearing a long white dress that came down to her feet. She walked to the window away from him. She seemed to glide there.

"Beautiful night, isn't it Frank?" she asked, staring outwards.

"I want to know what you're doing here?" he asked in return.

He took a couple of steps towards her. "I was told I was to be alone."

"You were told by whom?"

"By Mr. Williams."

"By who?"

"Mr. Williams! The man that owns this place!" he screamed.

"I'm sorry. I don't know any Mr. Williams," she said.

"Stop playing games with me, lady! How else did you get in here? What would you be doing here if you don't know Mr. Williams?" Bonner yelled, in frustration.

"I assure you, I don't know him."

She came over and touched the organ; not so close as to be very close to him. "I only know my music. I came here to play my music, in solitude, to practice. That's all. To not be bothered by anyone; to better myself."

"I still find it strange that an attractive girl would be all alone out here in the middle of the night playing an organ!" he said.

He looked at her he took another step in the room. "Okay. How did you get here? Did you walk?"

"I'm here aren't I?"

"Yes, you're here, but why?"

Bonner saw a table in the middle of the room. He turned the flashlight upside down so it's beacon would shine on the ceiling helping to light the room, but not by much.

He looked at her again. "I was supposes to spend the night alone in this castle; by myself. He owns this place, this Mr. Williams. He bet me five hundred dollars that I couldn't stay here and come out alive. I told him to 'up his' and I'll take him up on it. I mean, what's to staying overnight in a dump?; the easiest five hundred dollars I ever made!" Bonner said, confidently.

"Seems like a sure thing."

"Sure thing? It's like *stealing!* I felt as if I was taking advantage of the old geezer. But those are the breaks; it's his money, and if he wants to part with it so easily that's his business."

He looked her. "And you, Missy; not that I'm complaining, but having you here is a bonus; makes getting through the night a lot easier."

He sat in a chair near the door.

She returned to the organ and sat in the seat.

"What would you like to hear, Frank. I know a lot of songs," she said, arranging song books in front of her.

"You wouldn't know it by what I've heard," Bonner said.

She started playing a tune; a different one.

He folded his arms and listened.

After she had finished playing he applauded.

"Bravo!"

He stopped applauding. "So you like your music."

"Yes."

"Where do you live?"

She fiddled with the organ keys.

"Oh, around."

"Don't play with me. Where?"

"You don't expect me to answer that now do you? We just met?"

"How long have you been coming here; doing this?"

"Years."

"Years? And to be undiscovered? I find that amazing!" Bonner said.

"You have to practice to be good, Frank. Want to hear some more?" she asked, smiling back to him.

"Play."

She started to play again. It was the same strange melodious song she had played in the beginning. He sat through the entire song. He had a strange expression on his face.

He looked at her. "You like that song, don't you?"

"I like it."

She turned to him suddenly. "Did you like it?"

"It's okay."

"You don't have to sit so far away."

There was a chair closer to her; a few feet; he moved to that.

She smelled good; but the fragrance was very familiar. It was the fragrance his wife used to wear!

"Where did you get that fragrance?" he asked.

"Oh, I got it?" she said.

It was all too familiar. He couldn't stand it.

"That's not an answer. Where did you get it?" he asked again, more demandingly

"You ask a lot of questions. Why not just enjoy the night?"

She played another song.

She looked back at him. "You like that?"

"Yes. You're very talented. But I'm not quite sold. There's something unusual, I mean, not quite right about a girl out in the middle of the night playing an organ," he said.

He placed his big hands on the organ keys. "Don't you think that's true, Loren? Loren what?"

Bonner seemed more determined.

She looked at him.

"Just Loren," she said.

She continued. "Okay. I'm from Chicago. I came here on a visit to see some relatives."

"Now we're getting somewhere," he said. "You play for relatives to?"

"Yes."

"Then why aren't you playing for them now?" he asked.

She turned away.

"I do. Sometimes. In fact, I play all over. I'm a bit of a concerto. I've played all over the northeast," she said.

"No kidding? I've never heard of you."

"You will, I'm still very young. There is time," she said.

"You want to do this? Is this your forte?"

"My what?"

"You know, your calling? Is this what you were meant to do?" he asked.

She played five or six more notes.

"I guess. It's what I enjoy," she concluded.

Want to hear another tune.

She played one and looked back to him. "How was that?"

"Okay. Different," he said, a bit more relaxed.

She turned towards the organ again.

"What about you?"

"Me?"

"Yes. What is your story?"

He seemed a bit caught off guard.

"Oh, there's not much to tell. I was born in Baltimore, as you know. I dropped out of school when I was fourteen. I moved around from place to place and eventually found a job working in a auto shop. I soon decided to leave town," he confessed.

"And here you are in this run down house with me. We are so much alike, Frank."

"In what way?"

"You're running away from a dream. I'm chasing one."

He looked disgusted. He stood up and walked away.

"You asked me to tell you my story, didn't you?"

"Yes."

"Then why are you telling it for me?!" he asked, becoming frustrated again.

"Because you must be in pretty bad shape to be taking a bet for five hundred dollars from a perfect stranger!" she answered.

"It's none of your business why I took the bet. Anyone would. You just keep practicing those songs on your organ and we'll get through this night, and you'll be better and I'll be richer," Bonner said.

"Fine Frank. I didn't mean to rile you," she said.

"You didn't. And I didn't mean to yell at you."

She stuck out her hand.

"Friends?"

He looked at her with a disgusted look.

"Little lady, I don't know what you're doing out here, but. . . "

He stuck out his hand to her. "Friends."

They shook hands.

He noticed her hands were as cold as ice.

He pulled away.

He looked at her. "Your hands, they're so *cold.*"

She pulled away.

She stood up, walked over to the open window and pulled it down.

She turned to him.

"I'm so used to being here. Must be the breeze," she said.

"Yeah, I suppose," Bonner said.

He saw many song books on top of the organ. He reached for them and pulled the stack into his hands.

He began thumbing through them. "You know all these songs?"

"Most of them," she answered.

"There sure are a lot of them. I guess that makes you versatile; a very talented person," he said.

"Oh, perhaps."

"I guess you must think I'm a bit of a heel for being out here for money?" he asked, still thumbing through the song books.

"No, not really," she said, while rubbing her arms. "I understand. Money is very important."

She walked over to the organ. She sat on top of it.

She looked at him. "So you do like my world?"

"I said you were talented, that's all," Bonner said.

"You're still here. After all you've seen and heard, you're still here."

"Yes, I'm still here. Where am I going this time of night?"

She rubbed the top of the organ gently.

"Most men would have turned away if they saw someone like me out in the middle of the night playing music," she said, without looking at him.

"I'm not like most men," he said.

She smiled at him in a strange way.

"I can believe that."

"What do you mean?"

"That you're not like most men. After all, you are still sitting here, aren't you?" she asked.

He stood up and came around to the side of the organ. He sat on top of it next to her. He put his arms around her and motioned towards her.

She pulled away and smiled at him in a gay manner. "Easy, Frank. We barely know each other."

She came over and gave him a quick peck on the lips. She fluffed his hair. He grabbed her like an animal.

She broke free of his grip. "Relax, Frank. We have all night, remember?"

She came to the back of him at the organ. She began to massage his shoulders. "You do have nice shoulders, Frank; wide; wider than I've ever seen on any man."

"I work out a lot."

"You do. Where?"

He looked in back at her.

"I thought you said you knew everything about me?"

"I do, Frank."

"Then how do you know I'd stand for this; this badgering me like this? How do you know I won't take advantage of you now? What do you want?" he asked.

"You, Frank. You."

"Me?"

"Yes. And I do know you. I do know all about you. Believe me."

He came to the other side of the organ and took her by both arms. "Lady you'd better talk."

"I know you've been a bad boy," she said.

She shook herself free from him again and walked away.

She looked back at him. "I know you've just escaped from prison; that you're on the lam and the authorities are looking for you. That's why you took this job; you're broke and you need money; quick money and this was a way to get it," she said.

". . . That I'm a sucker for beautiful women. . . especially one that knows all the answers?"

He looked at her and came closer. He went over to her and grabbed her again.

She walked away again.

He became amused. "You can dish it out, but you can't take it! Well anyone can tell you've been prompted for this! It's a performance! And I've exposed your little act!"

"I can take it, Frank," she said.

There was a bed in the corner of the room. She went over and sat on it. She extended both her arms to him.

He hesitated.

There were two glasses on the table next to her. The glasses were already filled. "How about a drink, Frank?"

He noticed the two glasses filled; two glasses exactly.

He became curious.

"How did you know to pour two glasses? They've been there all night, haven't they?" he asked.

"Let's just say, I was expecting you," she answered.

"Me? How could you possibly - ? We just met!"

She reached over took a glass and handed it to him.

"Drink up. Enjoy."

After a couple of seconds he reached across the room and took the glass. She took a sip from her glass. She reared her head back completely and started to laugh. But it wasn't a 'gayish' laughter; it was more of a knowing nature, one that drink or no drink, rubbed Bonner the wrong way.

He came over, ripped off the top of her blouse and pushed he back on the bed.

"Like I said, Missy; what's to stop me from taking advantage of you right now? We're a hundred miles from nowhere. I could have my way and lose five hundred dollars and no one would be the wiser. Who knows? You might even be worth it. Are you worth five hundred dollars?" he asked.

"I'd say so, Frank. But don't lose it. I would not want you to do that. Not yet," she said.

"Not yet?"

He sat up straight on the bed and took a sip from his glass.

"I'm not afraid of you, Frank. You're just a nice man who's gotten into a whole lot of trouble," she said.

She took the glass from him and sat it on the table. Then she sat her's next to him. She gave him another little kiss on his lips. Then she stood up and walked around the room humming a tune. It was the same tune he heard that caught his attention.

Bonner took notice.

"That's the same tune you were playing when I walked through that door! Why do you keep playing it?" he yelled.

"It's a nice tune isn't it?"

She went to the window in almost a dance. "It's a beautiful night, isn't it?"

"A beautiful night, for a beautiful girl," he said.

"Thank you, Frank. You flatter me, friend," she said.

"I'm not trying to flatter you. I'm just wondering why such a beautiful girl isn't home trying to get her beauty sleep, instead of frolicking around in the middle of the night humming strange tunes?" he asked.

"I can play it again, if you like?"

"Nevermind."

He came over to her at the window.

He picked her up and brought her back to the bed. He took off his shirt. "I'll leave that up to you. But I'm no toy, lady. So the game is over," he said.

"Does it matter, Frank? We're out here all alone."

'I'd just like to know who you are before I take full advantage of you?"

She started to humm the stange tune again in his ear.

He backed away. "Stop it!"

He closed his ears with his hands. "Stop it before I slap you!"

She worked her way from under him and went to the organ stool. She sat. She began to thumb through several music books.

"Let me see. It's here someplace."

"What?"

"The words. It's come back to me: I have the words!"

"I'm not interested."

"But Frank. You should hear it. It's for you, Frank."

"For me?"

"Yes."

Her eyes lit up. "Here it is!"

She placed the lead sheets on the organ.

She began to sing gayly.

'Oh, Frank Bonner,
you murdered your
wife,
your life was full
of strift,
you had a bad temper
it would have been
much simpler. . .
to give her a chance,
to rekindle your romance. . .
It could have
been gain
to let her explain,
but you beat
her to,
that is
so true
Oh Frank Bonner,
you murdered your wife!'

He stood up defiantly.

"It's a lie, I tell you! It's a lie! Where'd you get that?!" he yelled at her.

She looked across the organ at him.

"Give yourself up, Frank. You can run away from a lot of things but you can't run away from yourself!" she uttered.

"Shut up!"

"Go back to Baltimore."

He took the table where the glasses were and broke off one of it's legs.

He held it up.

"Shut or I'll shut you up!"

"Frank; sweet Frank. You're a good man. But you've had some tough breaks. Why did you do it? But now that you have you are trying to cover you tracks by running away. You think five hundred dollars is going to help you do that? It won't scratch the surface. *Give up,*" she said.

"Lady, I did it before and I'll do it again!"

He held the leg of the table even higher.

She started to sing, this time with the organ music:

'Oh,

Frank Bonner

you murdered your wife,

your life was full of strift,

You had a bad temper,

It would have been simpler,

to give her a chance,

to rekindle your romance,

It could have

been gain

To let her

explain,

but you

beat her to,
you know that
It's true!
Oh,
Frank Bonner
You murdered your wife!!!'
He dropped the leg of the chair and ran over to her. He grabbed her by both arms.
"Shut up! Shut up! Shut up!"
"Give up, Frank, baby! You can't run from your conscious!"

He began to hear the tune *over* and *over* in his head. Even when she was not playing it he heard it! He put his hands over his ears and began to wonder around the room. He beat the walls! He covered his ears and tried to block out any and all sounds but he could not stop from hearing the catchy tune; it echoed in his mind and it drove him to the limit. The room started to spin and he began to perspire.

Then, without looking at him she said; "It's all over, Frank. And here's the big finish!"

She began playing again: over and over.
'Oh,
Frank Bonner
You murdered your wife,
You're life was full
of strift,
You had a bad temper
It would have been
Simpler,
to give her a chance,
to rekindle your romance,
Your conscious will say,
You must now repay,
Oh,

Frank Bonner
you murdered your wife!!!'

She looked at him. "Give up, darling Frankie. You can't run from your conscious! Your conscious, Frank! YOUR CONSCIOUS!"

He dropped to his knees and recovered his ears.

"Stop   it!   Stop   it!   Shut   up! Ahhhhhhhhhhhhhhhhhhhhhhhhhhhhhhhhhhh!!!"

His ears were still covered by his hands.

He got up and bolted through the door yelling as he did. He ran down the long hallway and leaped through a window at the end. He plunged to the ground below, screaming every foot of the way as he did.

Chapter
Nine

T*he policeman* on the ground below was directing traffic around the man laying in the center of the busy Baltimore street.

It was a two lane road right in the center of town. People on both sides had stopped to stare, the scene had it's shares of looky-loos.

A lone man broke from the crowd and tapped the policeman on the shoulder.

"What happened here, Sir?" he asked the officer.

"Him? Oh, that's Frank Bonner the notorious escapee! He leaped off the fourth floor of the building right onto the concrete pavement, poor guy. Should have just turned himself in, or maybe at the very least taken the elevator. Maybe he'd just gotten away with just a life sentence," the officer answered.

The man walked away and stepped back into the crowd. The policeman continued to direct traffic as more officers arrived.

The End

DEAR READER:

Thank you for reading 'The House on the EDGE of Homerville! Won't you take a minute to post a brief, short, polite review? Honest reviews will help readers decide if they will enjoy a book. Again, thank you for the read and have a nice day!

Sincerely,

-the author-

-**WALT FOSTER HAS ALWAYS** been a fan of mysteries and science fiction and he loves to write them. He lives in the United States U.S.A.

Don't miss out!

Visit the website below and you can sign up to receive emails whenever Walter Foster publishes a new book. There's no charge and no obligation.

https://books2read.com/r/B-A-BRFW-SAJEC

Connecting independent readers to independent writers.

Did you love *The House on the Edge of Homerville*? Then you should read *FRAGMENTS: abort Martian landing!*[1] by Walter Foster!

[2]

"Mayday! Mayday! We're in trouble up here!" came a desparate voice from space.

One million two hundred thousand miles from Earth the *MARTIAN THREE* rocket to Mars began to break up and fall apart. No one knows why one of the finest rockets ever built began to shake and fall apart, only that the Martian landing is out of the question. Suddenly, the only thought is to devise a plan to get the three brave men safely back to Earth!

---

1. https://books2read.com/u/bW01p0

2. https://books2read.com/u/bW01p0

Also by Walter Foster

Blackula the Vampire!
Tour of Atlantis
The House on the Edge of Homerville
Blackenstein
FRAGMENTS: abort Martian landing!

About the Author

Walt Foster has always been a fan of mysteries and science fiction and he loves to write them. He lives in the United States U.S.A.